Monster Stew

Let's make Monster Stew!

Here is the fire, nice and hot,
to cook Monster Stew.

4

Here is the pot, big and black,

that sits on the fire, nice and hot,
to cook Monster Stew.

5

Here are two rocks.
Here are four leaves.

Here are six webs.

Here are eight shells.

Add them to the pot, big and black,

that sits on the fire, nice and hot,
to cook Monster Stew.

9

Here are ten sticks.
Here are twelve shoes.

Here are fourteen hats.

Here are sixteen socks.

Here are eighteen buttons.

Here are twenty pinecones.

Add them to the pot, big and black,

that sits on the fire, nice and hot,
to cook Monster Stew.

15

It's ready! Yum!